Toasting Marshmallows

Camping Poems

by Kristine O'Connell George
Illustrated by Kate Kiesler

Clarion Books ✳ New York

Clarion Books
a Houghton Mifflin Company imprint
215 Park Avenue South, New York, NY 10003

The illustrations were executed in acrylic paint.
The text was set in 16-point Goudy.
Book design by Janet Pedersen.

www.houghtonmifflinbooks.com

Printed in Singapore

Library of Congress Cataloging-in-Publication Data

George, Kristine O'Connell.
Toasting marshmallows : camping poems / by Kristine O'Connell George ; illustrated by Kate Kiesler.
p.   cm.
ISBN 0-618-04597-X
1. Camping—Juvenile poetry. 2. Children's poetry, American. [1. Camping—Poetry.
2. American poetry.] I. Kiesler, Kate, ill. II. Title.
PS3557.E488 T63 2001
811'.54—dc21   00-056984

TWP   10 9 8 7 6 5 4 3 2 1

For Mike,
for all our California, Colorado, Idaho, Utah,
and Wyoming "orange tent" memories
        —K. O'C. G.

For childhood friends Anne, Heidi,
Gareth, George, and Lee
        —K. K.

Tent

First,
smooth dirt.
No rocks or roots.
Next, sharp stakes, poles,
strong nylon rope. Shake, snap.
Billow, *whoof*, settle. Tug. Pull taut.
Our tent is up! Blooming, bright orange.

A Doe

Stepping timidly
out of the thicket,
she trembles, then stills,
    poised mid-quiver.

We don't move.
We don't even whisper.
She's almost
    close enough to touch.

Velvet ears swivel.
Slim spindled legs turn,
a silent shiver
    fading into dusk.

Scooter

At home, our dog snores
loose-boned, easy,
sprawled between
fireplace and couch,
losing himself
in tennis-ball dreams.

Here, by the campfire,
he's tightly coiled—
a thin, tense spring—
snarling into the night,
hackles lifting
his leather collar.

Tonight, Scooter
is Timber Wolf.

Campfire

Warm front. Cold back.
I turn around.
Warm back. Cold front.
I turn around.

I lean against Mom,
my head on her shoulder.
Warm all over.

Sleeping Bag

It's so cold outside,
I'm getting dressed inside
my sleeping bag.
I wriggle, *scoootch*,
scrunch, and jiggle. Flop.
Front flips, back flips—
I'm a caterpillar
in a cozy cloth cocoon
that zips.

Breakfast

This chipmunk
does not dine,
does not idle,
does not linger,
has no time
for chits and chats,
nibbling bits
of this and that.

Then, suddenly . . .

a chipmunk dash
    past my feet,
        a furry flash
            sneaks a piece,
races back,
    chewing fast,
        a pancake feast
            in chubby cheeks.

11

The Best Paths

The best paths
are whispers
in the grass,
a bent twig,
a token, a hint,
easily missed.

The best paths
hide themselves
until the right
someone
comes along.

The best paths
lead you
to where
you didn't know
you wanted to go.

Abandoned Cabin

Standing where the door once was,

I look inside.

Surprised to have a guest, something scurry-hides
in hasty scrambles to a hidden space
between the chinks of a crumbling fireplace.
The ceiling is sky blue, powdered with cloud.
Someone's entertaining an elegant crowd
of Queen Anne's lace. Bars of sun run across
the dirt floor carpeted in damp green moss.
Leaning in through the window, a pine bough.

There's more sky than cabin.
The forest lives here now.

By Myself

I might sit here all day,
      listening to aspen leaves ruffle,
      watching the quiet things,
      waiting to see what happens.

I might sit here all day
      until I see seventeen jays,
      until the beetle reaches the pine,
      until the panther cloud crosses the sky.

I might sit here all day
      by myself, alone,
      quiet and still,
      silent as stone.

Storm

Late in the afternoon
the wind begins to blow
whistle-sharp, wet and cold.
Whitecaps lace the lake.
Uneasy, the birds
dart from tree to tree
as heavy black clouds
rumble toward us,
an oncoming train
hauling a thunderous
load of storm.
Rain!

Rain Dance

It was dry
under these trees,
until a confetti of birds
in the wet leaves

danced
another
rain shower.

Mosquito Song

It's meeeeeeeeeeeeeeeeeeeeeee!

Mosqueeeeeeeeeeeeeeto!

Is that *you*, Dinner?

Greeeeeeeeeetings!

Toasting Marshmallows

I am a careful marshmallow toaster,
a patient marshmallow roaster,
turning my stick oh-so-slowly,
taking my time, checking often.
This is art—
a time of serious reflection
as my pillowed confection
slowly reaches golden perfection.

My brother
          grabs 'em with grubby hands
                    shoves 'em on the stick
                              burns 'em to a crisp
                                   cools 'em off
                                        flicks soot
                                             eats quick.

I'm still turning my stick.
He's already eaten *six*.

Two Voices in a Tent at Night

Shhhhh . . .
Something is scratching
on our tent.

Is not.

Is too.

Is not.

Scratching!

I don't hear anything.

Something is scratching!

Go to sleep.

It's you! Stop it!

No, it's *not*. It's a branch.

It is you!
Isn't it?

OK. OK. It *was* me . . .
Wait.
Something's scratching!
Listen.

Told you so.
Scratching!

Shhhhhh. Are *you* doing that?

No. No. No!

Think it's the dog?

I hope so.

Eavesdropping

Tipping
a slender
silver ear,
Moon tries
to pretend
she isn't
listening
to our
secrets.

Max's Bait Shop

Faded snapshots
of folks with the fish
they caught at this lake.

Talk is short here.
 Any luck?
 What's biting?
The lucky ones lie, saying:
 Well, not much.

Fishing lures powdered with dust,
 red and white floats,
 hand-tied flies

next to candy bars,
 stale potato chips,
 a jar of beef jerky.

Icebox with
 cheese sandwiches,
 sodas, and stuff—
 next to the worms
 in cardboard cups.

Gone Fishing

No one else was awake
when we got up at dawn
to go fishing.
Walking the steep path
down to the lake,
we could see the circle flop
and splash of trout. I warned
my little brother not to go
too close to the edge.
He said:

> *You can't tell **me** what to do.*

No one else was awake
when we got up at dawn
to go fishing. All I caught
was one little brother—
hauled up out of the cattails,
sputtering, soggy, and still stubborn.

Rowing to the Island

Mom and I row

      —and row
      and row—

leaving the shore
in our wake.

Such hard work,
pulling an island
across a lake.

Wild Mustard

Sweeps of wild mustard
swinging up the hillsides
as far as I can see.
      Yellow waltzes,
       yellow weaves,
       yellow invites me
to wade in, up to my knees.
      Yellow hums,
       yellow sings,
       yellow dances—
with dizzies of bees.

Forest Walk

I'm practicing my
      I-belong-here
      no-twig-snap
      no-leaf-rustle
      no-branch-crack
      see-all, know-all
      float-like-fog
      like-smoke
      pine-needle-soft
      forest walk.

No one will know I'm coming.
No one will know when I'm gone.

Cave

The cave breathes icy and ancient,
measuring time with slow drips
that echo as water hits granite
somewhere deep in this cavern.

We step over an underground stream
that carved hollow pools,
      filled with strange, pale fish
      swimming blind up black passages
      in this alien underground land.
I hold my breath,
      slip my chilled fingers
      into Dad's warm hand.

Old Truck

Just off the path
       is a '54 GMC flatbed
       with four flat tires
       tightly wedged
       with heavy rocks
       and cinderblocks.
They're stiff,
       but the doors aren't locked
       on an old truck
       who's going nowhere again.
Her chrome grille
       is a shy, wistful grin.
       Her fading green paint
       peels in rusty scabs.
My brother and I climb
       into the dusty cab,
       pat her cracked seats,
       stow our gear.
Wonder who
       left her here
       high on this mountain,
       broken-down, alone.
       Guess it's up to us
       to drive her home.

Moose Brunch

A moose couldn't care less
that tourists stop to gawk,
back up traffic for miles.

Broad-shouldered, hump-backed,
an awkward scaffold halfway
between a camel and a horse,
with a bit too much of everything.

A moose couldn't care less—
just don't come too close—
he's content to stand
knobby-knee-deep
among the river reeds,
dunking his huge head,
munching daintily
on wet green weeds.

River Messages

River words run
     in scallops and scribbles,
scrolls of eddies
     and watery ripples.

I throw a pebble,
     skip a telegram
across the river,
     which never stops . . .

River writes,
     river talks:
Someone upstream
     is throwing rocks.

Flashlight

Dark night, rocky path,
flashlight beam shows me the way:
a round stepping stone.

Green bug on my book
pushing his long, important
shadow up the page.

Inside the flashlight—
round beam, one wide-open eye
staring back at me.

The bobbing circle
of light coming up the path,
bringing my father.

40

Owl

I hear you, Owl.
Your one lone vowel
drops like a stone
in night's dark pond,
    an almost-echo
    funnels round,
    a hollow sound.

I hear you, Owl.
The wind rush
of your wings
shouldered and spread,
    pleating the night,
    the satin flap
    of your feathered cape.

Owl? I hear you.
I'm awake, too.

Sleeping Outside

Small me,
in a small tent
staked to a huge planet,
rolling slowly through open space—
alone.

Small me,
still wide awake
under a wide starred sky,
almost—*almost*—feeling the earth
turning.

Anchored

Outside our tent I can see
    gray spiders spinning silver,
        looping silky lines
through smoky wisps
    of campfire, coffee steam,
        and early morning mist—
an aerial tramway stretching
    bright and high into the tree,
        firmly anchoring our tent.

We will have to stay
at least one more day.

Pulling Up Stakes

The fire is doused,
the coals are cold,
the tent collapsed,
the car packed.

I find two rocks—
    one to keep,
    one to hide,
        in my secret place,

        to say: *I was here*,
        to say: *I'll be back next year*.

Flannel

Red and blue plaid,
pockets with buttons,
my camping shirt
is flannel, worn soft,
pine smells, campfire,
forest moss.

I keep it hidden
in my bottom drawer—
where no one will find it
and wash away
my memories.